HADLEY HAD

Written and Illustrated by

Adam Paslay

Over the ocean

and across the land

a turtle buries

her eggs in the sand.

So full of joy to see
what her babies will be

counting the days until they
return to the sea.

With no time to waste

the turtles make haste

breaking their shells

to get out of that place.

With their little turtle feet

making little

turtle tracks.

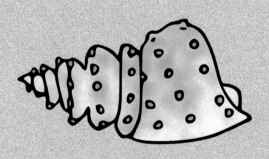

Instead of the ocean.
One turtle crawls to land.
That's where this little
turtle's story began.

-7-

"This place is so big" exclaimed our little adventurer.

"Wow! I had never seen such a thing before."

"I think I'll call you...Hadley"

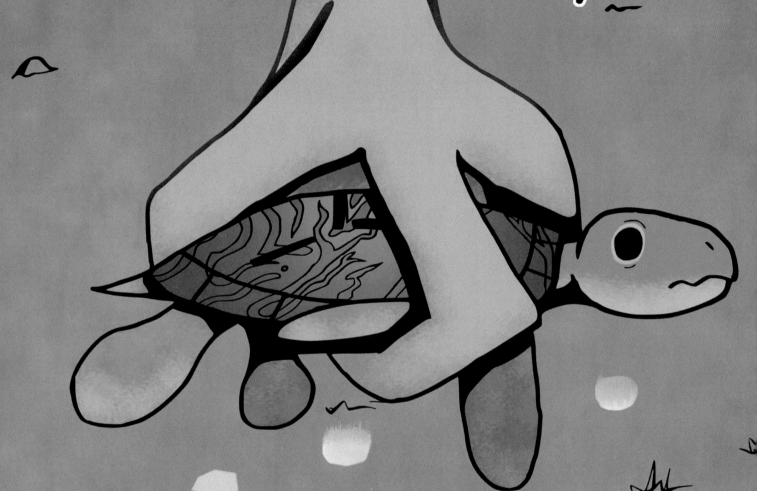

So our duo had
made it to a cliff.
Salt in the air
but only a whiff.

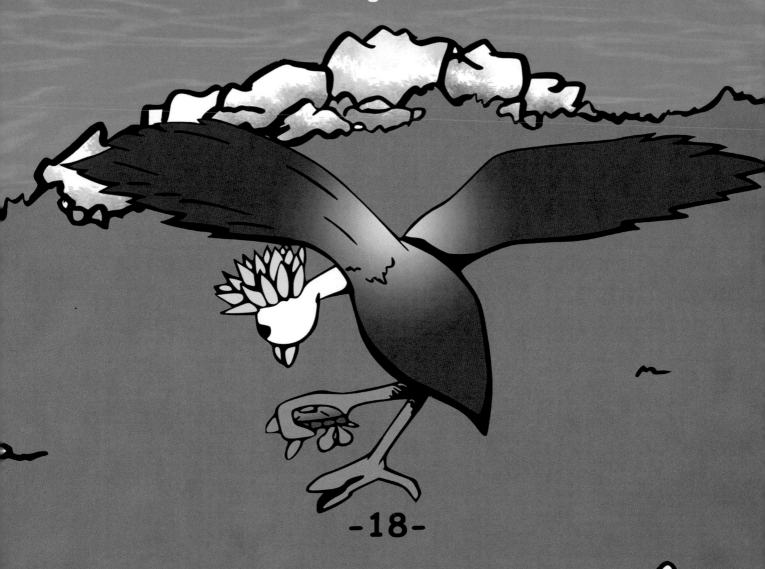

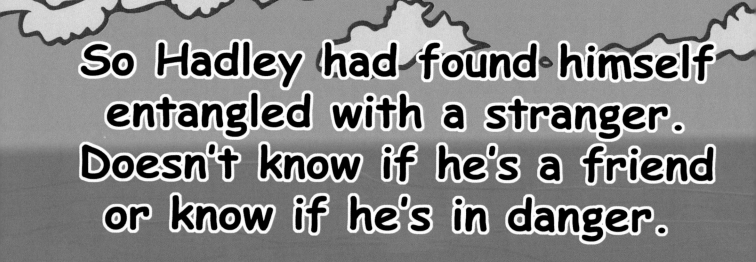

So Hadley had found himself entangled with a stranger. Doesn't know if he's a friend or know if he's in danger.

For a moment Hadley
had felt so free.

The wind on his face and
the smell of the sea.

A beautiful day and nice clear weather.

Flapping his wings to realize he has no feathers.

No need to fret over a few
scrapes and tumbles.

A mistake here and there
is what makes us humble.

"I have never seen a bird that could not fly." chuckled the bird.

"You are lucky it was a small cliff. Well let's try it again."

"I don't believe
I am a bird"
says Hadley.

"Also I don't think these are wings. I think I must go" Hadley groans.

So Hadley had ventured through the trees once more.

Then he came
across a noise.

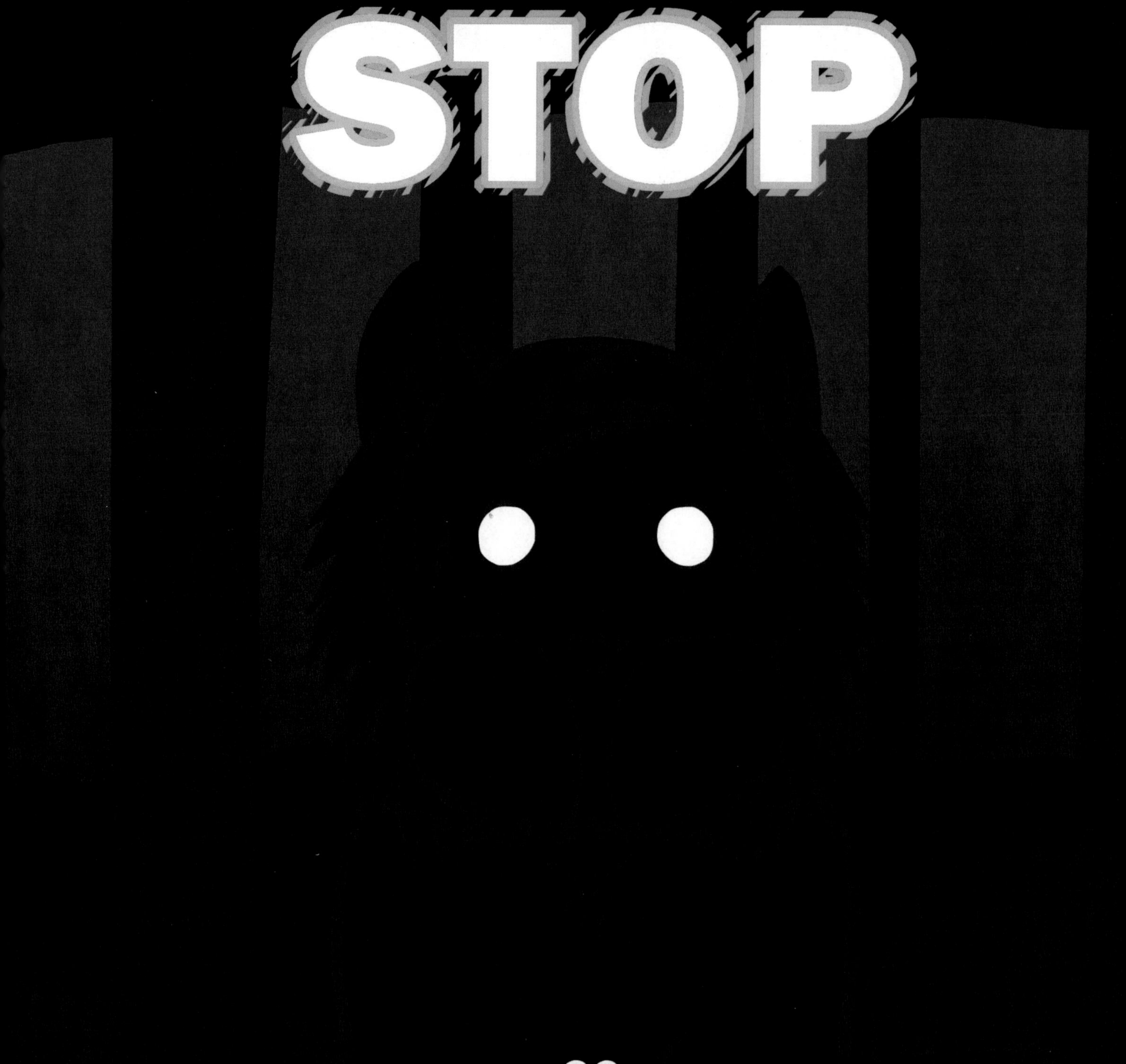
STOP

You don't smell like a pig.

"You don't taste like a rabbit." growled the tiger.

"You hear that?
The sound of the jungle.
You feel that?
The soul of the forest."
the tiger muttered.

"All I can feel are rocks.
The sand is much softer.
Maybe I'll feel it when
I pounce."
Hadley pointed out.

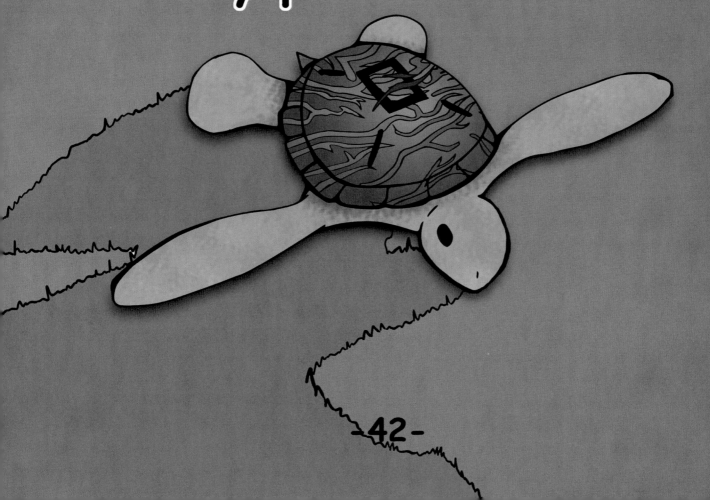

The tiger whispers,"See there
It's our lunch. Lay low, hold
your breath and...

He feels his arms are not
made for jungles,
a few steps and he tumbles.

His journey is all his own,
to venture out,
into the unknown.

-48-

"Well my stripes are not as bold as yours are, and everyone gets scars. I do not think I am a tiger."

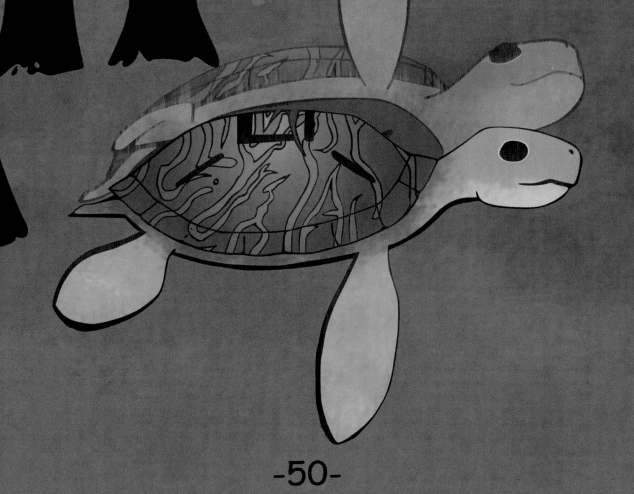

So Hadley had made it
to the sand.
As he came across
a small creature
on the land.

So Hadley approaches and asked "What are you?"

"Well I am snail." he replied.

"I think I am a snail too."
Hadley says excitedly.

"You are not a snail"
he replied.

"But I have a shell like you and I'm slow like you. I must be a snail." Hadley sighed.

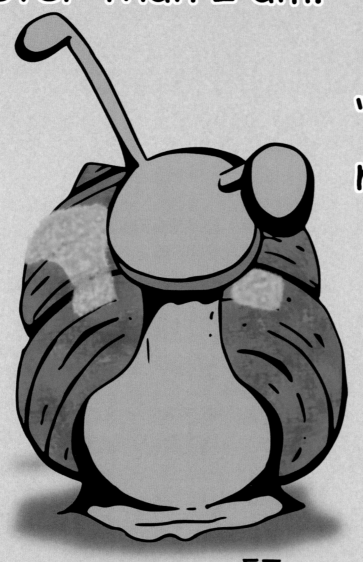

"I don't know what I am."
Hadley said.

"Yeah you do. You have seen it.

You have heard it.

It calls out to you.

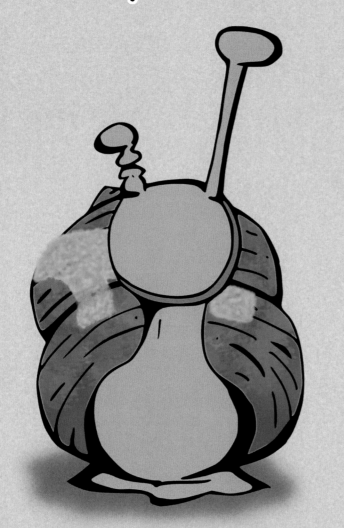

What's been calling you?"

"The salt. The sand. The ocean. Yeah the ocean keeps calling me." Hadley realized.

"Well then there you go.
Go to the ocean."
the snail said as
he waved goodbye.

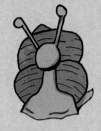

Hadley had then realized that he could fly under the water.

That he could pounce under the sea

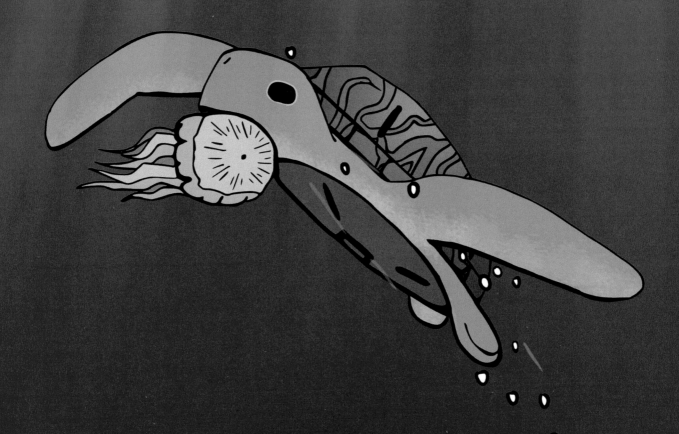

because Hadley had found,
the place he needed to be.

Born in Texas but raised in a Puerto Rican household. Adam provides a unique perspective that only a multicultural person can bring. His love of animals and art are definitely reflected in his work.